Spells & Potions

KATE RIGGS

CREATIVE EDUCATION

COPYRIGHT

Published by Creative Education
P.O. Box 227, Mankato, Minnesota 56002
Creative Education is an imprint of
The Creative Company
www.thecreativecompany.us

Design by Stephanie Blumenthal
Production by Christine Vanderbeek
Art direction by Rita Marshall
Printed in the United States of America

Photographs by Alamy (AF archive, Corbis Flirt, INTERFOTO, Moviestore collection Ltd), Dover Publications Inc. (Children's Book Illustrations), Graphic Frames (Agile Rabbit Editions), Shutterstock (img85h), SuperStock (Newberry Library, Universal Images Group)

Illustration page 5 © 1983 Monique Felix; illustration page 13 © 1984 Etienne Delessert

Library of Congress Cataloging-in-Publication Data
Riggs, Kate.
Spells & potions / by Kate Riggs.
p. cm. — (Happily ever after)
Summary: A primer of the familiar fairy-tale devices of spells and potions, from who uses them to their effects upon recipients, plus famous stories and movies in which they have appeared.
Includes index.
ISBN 978-1-60818-244-2
1. Charms—Juvenile literature. 2. Incantations—Juvenile literature. I. Title.

GR600.R54 2013
133.4'4—dc23   2011051175

First edition
9 8 7 6 5 4 3 2 1

TABLE OF CONTENTS

"*Once upon a time,
there was a **wicked** witch who made
potions. She cast a spell on a princess.*"

Spells and potions are things you
can find in fairy tales. A fairy tale
is a story about magical people
and places.

Fairy tale characters cast spells to get something they want. A bad witch may cast a **curse**. A good fairy may cast a spell to protect someone.

Potions are magical drinks. They can be used to make people fall in love. They can be used to heal a sick person. But they can also be used to hurt people or turn them into animals.

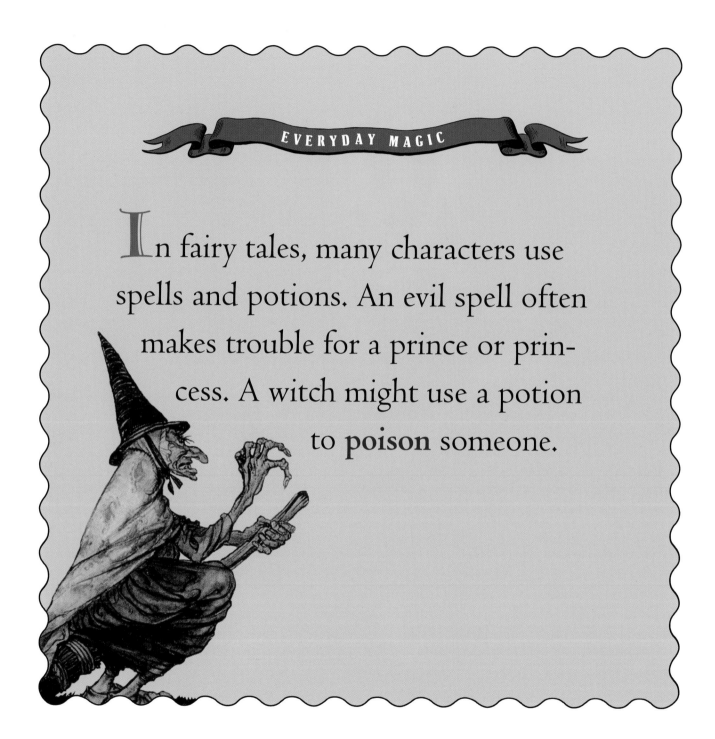

EVERYDAY MAGIC

In fairy tales, many characters use spells and potions. An evil spell often makes trouble for a prince or princess. A witch might use a potion to **poison** someone.

∽ II ∾

Spells can trap people inside enchanted castles. Sometimes a spell or potion can change someone into a magical creature. Or a spell can turn an everyday object into something new, like a shoe into a glass slipper.

Loving someone or doing something good is the best way to break a bad spell. Spells do not last forever. The magic runs out. Then everything returns to normal.

In the fairy tale *The Little Mermaid*, a young mermaid falls in love with a human prince. She asks a witch for a potion that will turn her into a human. The witch gives her the potion. But the Little Mermaid has to give up her voice.

The story *Cinderella* is about a girl who asks her fairy godmother for help. The fairy godmother casts spells to help Cinderella go to a ball. There she meets a prince, and the two fall in love.

THE END

Once a bad spell is broken, everyone can be happy again!

"The princess was trapped in an enchanted castle for 50 years. Then her prince came and saved her. And everyone lived happily ever after."

Copy this short story onto a sheet of paper.
Then fill in the blanks with your own words!

Once upon a time, there was a prince named _____. He lived in a castle far away in the Land of _____. The prince was _____. He did not have _____. He asked a witch for a _____ potion. The potion changed him into a _____ instead! One day, a princess came to the prince's castle. She _____. The spell was broken! And they lived happily ever after.

GLOSSARY

curse—a spell that makes something bad happen

enchanted—put under a spell

poison—something that can hurt or kill a person

potions—magical drinks

wicked—bad or evil

READ MORE

Kurti, Jeff. *Disney Villians: The Top Secret Files*. New York: Disney Enterprises, 2005.

Perrault, Charles, and Roberto Innocenti. *Cinderella*. Mankato, Minn.: Creative Editions, 2000.

WEB SITES

Little Mermaid Crafts & Recipes
http://family.go.com/disney/pkg-disney-character-fun/pkg-disney-princess-ariel/
Have fun making crafts and treats that go along with the story of *The Little Mermaid*.

Match Cinderella's Shoes
http://www.northcanton.sparcc.org/~ptk1nc/cinderella/shoematch.html
Play this matching game to uncover the hidden picture.

INDEX